MARTIN LUTHER KING, JR.
A Biography for Young Children

MARTIN LUTHER KING, JR.
A Biography for Young Children

By Carol Hilgartner Schlank and Barbara Metzger

Illustrations by
John Kastner

gryphon house

Mt. Rainier, MD

This book was originally published by the Rochester Association for the Education of Young Children who wishes to acknowledge the assistance of the following organizations in making the publication of this book possible:
New York State Martin Luther King, Jr. Commission
Eastman Kodak Company
Daisy Marquis Jones Foundation
Barbara Merrill Memorial Fund of the Rochester Area Foundation

Published by Gryphon House, Inc., 3706 Otis Street, Mt. Rainier, Maryland 20712. 1 (800) 638-0928

This book is dedicated
to those educators and parents
committed to creating
the non-violent and peaceful world
Martin Luther King, Jr.
envisioned.

Many years ago on a cold winter day, Martin Luther King, Jr. was born. Mother Dear and Daddy King were proud and happy. Baby Martin's grandmother loved to hold and rock him.

Baby Martin soon grew to be a friendly lively little boy.
He played with his big sister, Christine, and his little brother, A. D.

Mother Dear wanted her children to be smart. She taught Christine, Martin, and A. D. to read when they were small. Martin loved to read his books.

Daddy King was a minister in the church down the street.
He wanted his children to be good. But Martin could not be good
all the time. Sometimes he got into big trouble with his father!

Mother Dear and Daddy King were often busy, but Grandmother always seemed to have time for Martin. He loved to sit in her lap. They talked together and shared secrets. She was Martin's favorite person.

Every Sunday Martin and his family got dressed up and walked down the street to the church where Daddy King was minister. Daddy King and the people prayed and sang. When Martin was small, he sang with the church choir, too.

Martin played ball and hide and seek with children in the neighborhood. He and his friends also loved to ride their bikes.

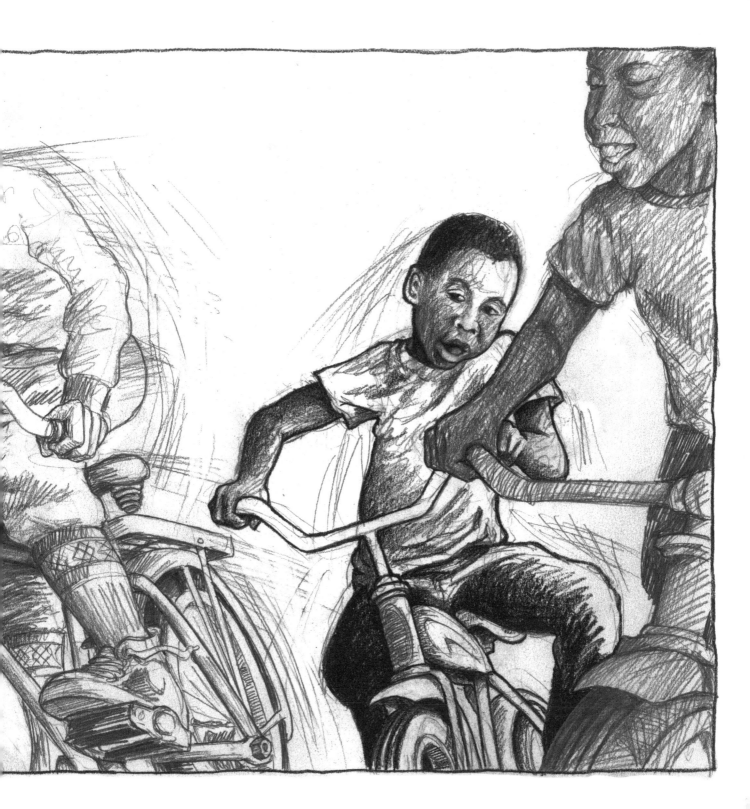

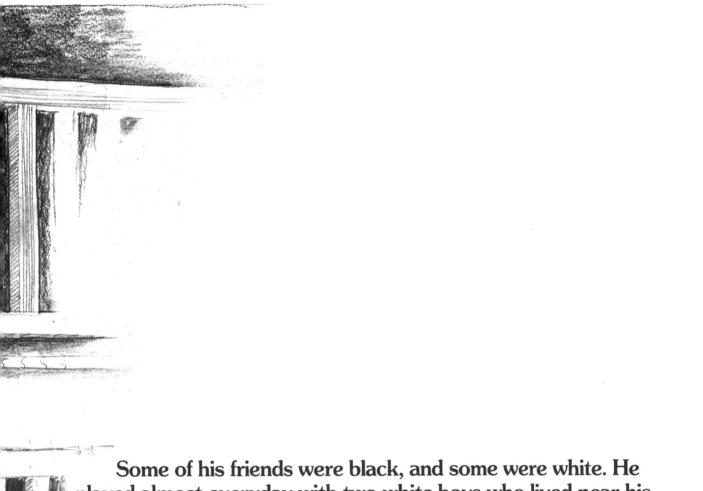

Some of his friends were black, and some were white. He played almost everyday with two white boys who lived near his house. But then, one awful day his friends' mother told the boys, "You can't be friends anymore, because Martin is colored, and you are white."

Martin ran home. "<u>Why</u> can't I be their friend?" he asked. His mother held him close. "Now that you are going to school, you can no longer be friends. You have to go to a school for our people, and they go to a school for white children."

She explained to him that many white people believed they were better than black people. "But," she said, "that is a lie."

Martin worked hard in school. He loved to learn new things. He wanted to know the answers to many questions. One big question he kept thinking about was how black and white people could be together and be friends.

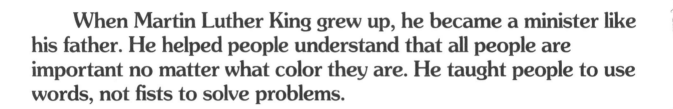

When Martin Luther King grew up, he became a minister like his father. He helped people understand that all people are important no matter what color they are. He taught people to use words, not fists to solve problems.

Martin Luther King had a dream that someday all people could learn to love and help each other. We celebrate his birthday every year because he worked so hard to make that dream come true.

J. KRASZNER